Raggedy Ann's Candy Heart Wisdom

Raggedy Ann's Candy Heart Wisdom

♥

Words of Love and Friendship

from the works of
Johnny Gruelle

SIMON & SCHUSTER BOOKS FOR YOUNG READERS

"A candy heart is very nice . . .
but one can be just as nice
and happy and full of sunshine
without a candy heart."

"Happiness is very easy
to catch when we
love one another and
are sweet all through."

"When one has pleasant thoughts
running through one's head,
one just has to be full of joyousness
and the joyousness shines right up to the
surface in a cheery smile."

"Very often we do not know
how many creatures and even people
do kind things for us in quiet ways."

"Every time we make a new friend,
it is just like planting another flower
in a beautiful garden filled with
the flowers of friendship."

"For every speck of fun
you give another,
you receive an echo
of that fun yourself."

"Many of the sweetest and most beautiful flowers grow from the ugliest little seeds, and we can never judge anyone until we know what is in his heart."

"If anyone sees a frown upon the face of a little boy or girl, all she has to do is place a cheery, smiley, loving kiss right on top of the frown, and the frown always leaves and a smile takes its place."

"Those who are unselfish may
wear rough clothes, but inside
they are always beautiful . . .
and reflect to others the happiness
and sunny music within their hearts."

"It always fills us with happiness
when we know we are truly loved
by one we dearly love."

"The more you give away,
the more you have yourself."

"It is very easy to find fault
with others instead of finding
out what the truth is about them."

"We should always feel and know that the sun is shining above the darkest of rain clouds and that with the passing of the rain, we shall see the gleaming of the rainbow."

"... how easy it is to pass over
the little bumps of life
if we are happy inside."

"When love fills our hearts,
happiness is everlasting."

"It is not how we look
that is important.
What really counts is
to be as sunny as possible inside;
then no one stops long
to look at the outside."

JOHNNY GRUELLE

"If we want others to be kind to us,
first we must do kind things for them."

"When you meet anyone, just stop and think, 'How can I show this person that I am a friend?' A little teeny voice inside you will tell you just how you can do it."

Simon & Schuster Books for Young Readers
An imprint of Simon & Schuster Children's Publishing Division
1230 Avenue of the Americas, New York, New York 10020
Copyright © 1999 by Simon & Schuster, Inc.
The names and depictions of Raggedy Ann and Raggedy Andy are trademarks of Simon & Schuster.

Individual copyrights for text:
Marcella Stories: Copyright © 1929 by John B. Gruelle, copyright renewed 1956 by Myrtle Gruelle; pp. 31, 38, 63.
Raggedy Andy Stories: Facsimile Edition Copyright © 1993 by Macmillan Publishing Company; "The Nursery Dance," p. 4; "The Taffy Pull," p. 7; and "The Singing Shell," p. 6.
Raggedy Ann and the Golden Ring: Copyright © 1961 by The Bobbs-Merrill Company, Inc.; p. 50.
Raggedy Ann and the Happy Meadow: Copyright © 1960 by The Bobbs-Merrill Company, Inc.; pp. 41, 53, 59, 65, 86.
Raggedy Ann's Lucky Pennies: Copyright © 1932 by John B. Gruelle; pp. 16, 94.
Raggedy Ann's Magical Wishes: Copyright © 1928 by Johnny Gruelle, copyright renewed 1956 by Myrtle Gruelle; pp. 28, 79.
Raggedy Ann and Raggedy Andy's Very Own Fairy Stories: Copyright © 1917 by P. F. Volland Company, copyright renewed 1945 by Myrtle Gruelle, copyright ©1949 by The Johnny Gruelle Company; pp. 58-59.
Raggedy Ann Stories: Facsimile Edition Copyright © 1993 by Macmillan Publishing Company; "Raggedy Ann's Trip on the River," p. 6.

All rights reserved including the right of reproduction in whole or in part in any form.
SIMON & SCHUSTER BOOKS FOR YOUNG READERS is a trademark of Simon & Schuster.
Printed and bound in the United States of America
First Edition 10 9 8 7 6 5 4 3 2 1
ISBN 0-689-82485-8
Library of Congress Catalog Card Number: 98-85868